13

THE CHRISTMAS TEDDY BEAR

Written and illustrated
by Ivan Gantschev

Text adapted
by Andrew Clements

A Michael Neugebauer Book

North-South Books / New York / London

Ellen and her mother arrived to visit Grandma and Grandpa two days before Christmas.
Grandpa met them at the station and bundled them up in the sled. It took almost an hour to get from the town out to the big estate, but there was no hurry, and there was plenty to talk about.

Ellen loved arriving at Butterfield. She felt like the granddaughter of a king whenever she came to visit.
Grandpa always said, "Now remember, Ellie, I'm just the caretaker here." But that didn't matter to her.

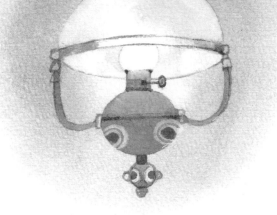

The caretaker's cottage was full of Christmas smells—a bowl of oranges on the table in the hall, the fir tree in the living room, and a plum pudding in the kitchen. Ellen gave her grandmother a big hug and then took a long ride on the rocking horse Grandpa had made for her two years ago. There was no room for it in their small house in the city, so Ellen rode it when she came to visit. Grandma said, "I keep it here in the kitchen so I can think about you every day."

Ellen went to bed early, and after she finished saying her prayers, she fell asleep and dreamed of the teddy bear that she hoped to get on Christmas morning.

The next morning Grandma was out of sugar, so Grandpa put on his coat. He asked, "Do we need anything else from town?" Mother said she needed some thread, and then she said, "Will you see if you can find a teddy bear for Ellen? I know it's what she wants, but when I went to buy one, the toy shop had none left." Grandpa laughed. "You leave it to me. If there's a teddy bear anywhere in town, I'll find it."

On the long walk to town, Grandpa thought about all the Christmas mornings he had seen in his life—more than seventy! And he could still remember so clearly the time when his own mother and father had given him a teddy bear. He could see that bear's black shiny eyes, and the bright red hat his mother had put on its head. He chuckled and thought, "Yes, there's nothing quite like a new teddy bear."

Everyone in town was bustling about, and
Grandpa bustled too. He bought the sugar at the
grocery, the thread at the button shop, and best of all, he found a
nice big teddy bear at the toy shop. Then, just for fun, he bought
a bright red cap and pulled it onto the bear's head. With all his
errands done, he ate a little lunch and then headed for home.

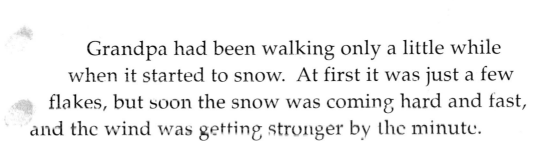

Grandpa had been walking only a little while
when it started to snow. At first it was just a few
flakes, but soon the snow was coming hard and fast,
and the wind was getting stronger by the minute.

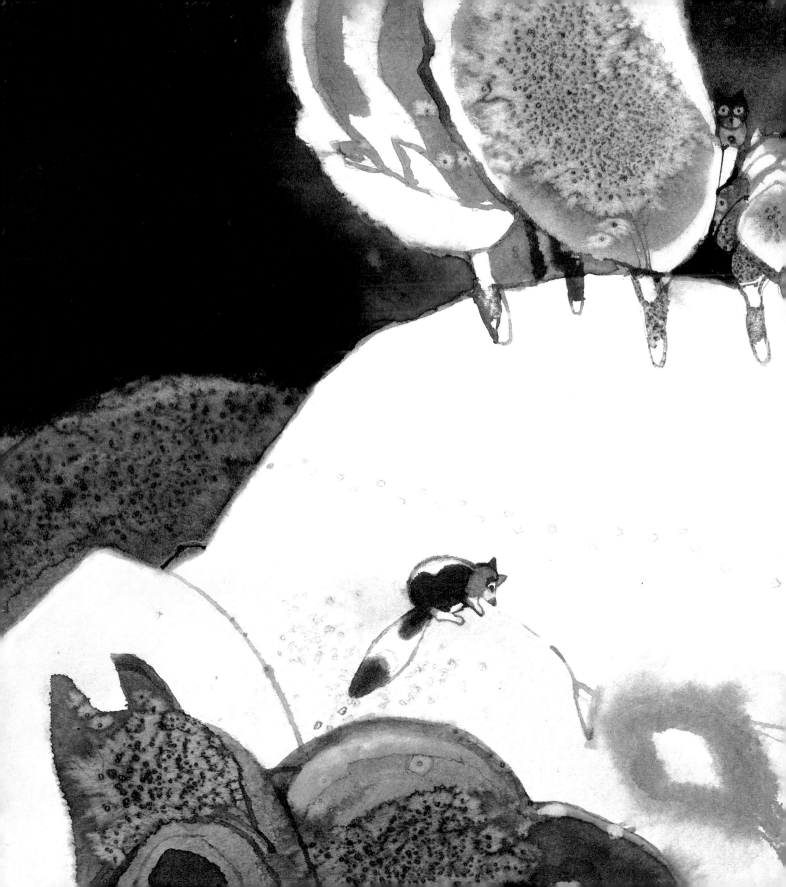

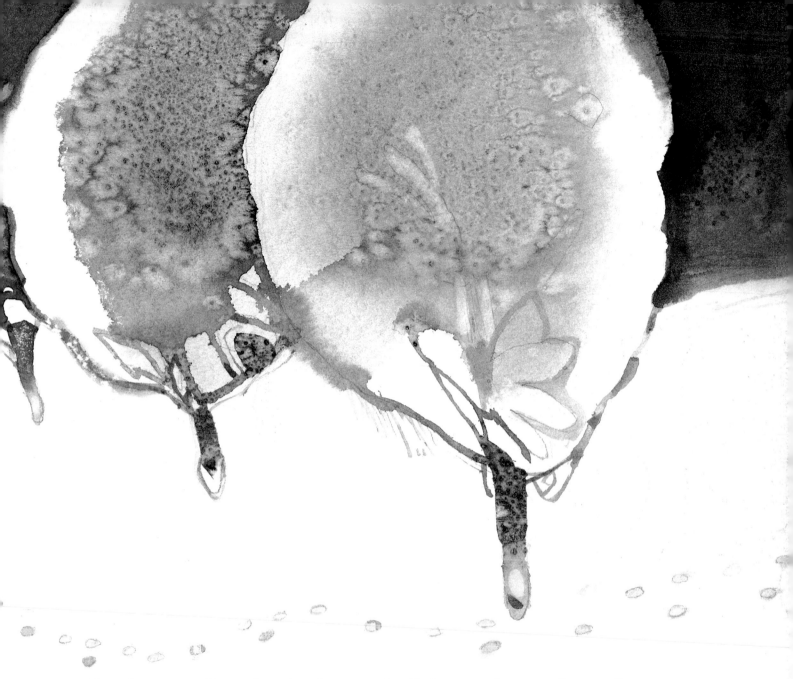

By the time Grandpa had turned off the road onto the path through the woods, it was snowing so hard that his footprints were filled in and covered up almost before he took the next step. The whipping wind and the blowing snow made it hard to see. Before long Grandpa was lost.

It started to get dark, and Grandpa still had not returned. Grandma was worried, so she asked some friends for help. They brought their lanterns and went out to search for Grandpa. Ellen's job was to ring the bell at the chapel so Grandpa could hear it and know which way to walk through the storm.

They searched for many hours.
It was getting very dark, and as
the snow stopped, it began to get colder.
They needed to find Grandpa soon.

Suddenly the gardener thought he saw someone
just at the edge of the lantern's light.

It was the teddy bear, and in the snow underneath
was Grandpa, very cold but still alive.

They helped him up, and together they walked
towards the sound of the chapel bell.

A short while later Grandpa was in bed sipping hot soup. Ellen was in bed too, for she had become very cold and tired from ringing the bell.
Her mother had tried to make her come down, but she had stayed there until Grandpa was back safe and sound.

Everyone
fell asleep early,
all except one damp little teddy bear.
He sat near the fir tree all night long with his shiny eyes wide open,
waiting for a wonderful Christmas day.

First published in the United States and Canada in 1994 by North-South Books,
an imprint of Nord-Süd Verlag AG, Gossau Zurich, Switzerland.

Copyright © 1992 by Michael Neugebauer Verlag AG
First published in Switzerland under the title Der Weihnachtsteddybär
by Michael Neugebauer Verlag AG, Gossau Zurich, Switzerland.

All rights reserved. No part of this book may be reproduced or utilized in any form
or by any means, electronic or mechanical, including photocopying, recording, or any information
storage and retrieval system, without permission in writing from the publisher.

Published in Great Britain, Australia, and New Zealand in 1992 by Picture Book Studio.
Reprinted in 1994 by North-South Books.

Distributed in the United States by North-South Books Inc., New York

Library of Congress Cataloging-in-Publication Data is available
A CIP catalogue record for this book is available from The British Library
ISBN 1-55858-349-1 (trade binding)
ISBN 1-55858-348-3 (library binding)
10 9 8 7 6 5 4 3 2 1
Printed in Belgium